The Popcorn House

Teamwork Makes the Dream Work

www.looklikeme.co.uk

Written by W. F. Duncan

& The Look Like Me Book Challenge Authors

Published in United Kingdom by the Look Like Me Book Challenge LTD, 2020.

www.looklikeme.co.uk & www.peachespublications.co.uk

British Library Cataloguing in Publication Data: A catalogue record for this book is available from the British Library.

Look Like Me Book Challenge LTD,

Kemp House, 160 City Road,

London, EC1V 2NX.

ISBN: 9781838147204

Book cover design: Look Like Me Book Challenge.

Editor and Typesetter: Winsome Duncan.

Proof reader and Critical Friend: Joanna Oliver.

Table of Contents

Dedication

To Brother Bear Ty, aka Ben Chijioke, thank you for the music. Rest in Power, King!

Thank You to our Seed Donors for Supporting Us

Acknowledgements

To the most-high God, thank you for your favour and mercies, which are renewed every morning. I have done what you instructed me to do; let there be less of me and more of you. Thy will be done.

To my fabulous, awesome team who have had my back every step of the way during this process; we smashed it. Thank you for believing in my vision in its infancy. You all have worked so hard and will be greatly rewarded in the months that will ensue. Shout out to Lescha Marshall, Vinessa Brant, Neusa Catoja, Miriam Manderson, Ben Lee, Jennette Arnold OBE, Sam-Jay Robinson and our Ambassadors, Anna Sexton and Adam Bradford. You rock and are the 'realest' foot soldiers. Let's go higher, higher in the words of Ty #upwards.

To our fabulous seed donors, we could not have hit our £1,000 goal without you. It took us ten months but we got there in the end and for that, I will be forever grateful. Look at what you have bloomed?

Joanna Oliver, you are an anomaly, always striving for quality assurance. Thank you dear heart, for being our Proof reader and friend. Look at what we have created & we did good, don't you think? Many thanks to Veronica Martin, for making me believe that I can hit our target of £50k and giving me complimentary funding consultancy, throughout the process. LinkedIn gave us the ultimate Link Up; you are a true blessing. Crystal Swain-Bates, thank you for your guidance.

Of course, I cannot forget our 30 budding child authors, which included my twin nephews, and all of the dedicated parents who brought together their tribe, to participate over a 3-month period, for this ground-breaking and historic project, 'The Popcorn House'.

A special thanks goes out to The Voice Newspaper, for championing our cause commercially.

Foreword

Winsome Duncan's passion for books is infectious. I met her in the capacity of Peaches Publications, where I had personally received one-to-one Book Confidence Coaching, for my own book with Winsome. A peach is sweet and an endearing fruit. They come from a seed and a seed is exactly what Winsome and her team have sown in 'The Popcorn House' narrative.

As a secondary school Headteacher, I know that organising 30 children for a workshop takes some planning. I was honoured to be asked to give the keynote speech at the very first, historic, Look Like Me Book Challenge workshop.

Children are the future and we need to act now to support and encourage them. The entire session was led online via Zoom video calls and was so artistically done, that I was drawn into staying and participating for two consecutive workshops. I took great pleasure in sharing my Power-Point presentation about cultural identity and the importance of our family tree, within the group.

My own pre-teen reading materials contained characters such as 'Topsy and Tim'. The stories in and of themselves were great, however they did lack equal representation, as there was always something missing. Me. Could I even feature as a character of a story?

There could not be a more poignant time than now, for 'The Popcorn House' to be launched. The collection of identities, with their wonderful characters and magical missions, makes this book an exciting exploration for all children of any background.

The opportunity of an open-door, benefits children of colour to see themselves and others that 'look like them' as the main characters, for an impactful change. It may sound strange, however in the eyes of a child, there begins a new appreciation of who they can become, as we all know, stories fuel inspiration. This has been demonstrated in the success of the box office smash, 'Black Panther'. Imagination helps us to believe. Our belief underpins who we become. We become, what we aspire to be. We cannot be, what we do not see.

Brought together by Winsome Duncan, I feel very honoured and proud to be included in her team, who worked together to grow the seeds of greatness from the 'Look Like Me Book Challenge'.

The Popcorn House is a ground-breaking book. I say this because it is a book created out of the minds of children, for children. It is a book, birthed out of a passion and a desire to make the world a better place. It is a book seeded out of Winsome's vision, with the tenacity to embrace the quote from Whitney, 'I believe the children are the future' and ensure that they leave their legacy in this positive story.

Winsome and her 30 young budding authors, bring us into a world of 'Kalaria', a fantasy that every child would be thrilled to be part of. Take in every single word, enjoy the rhyme play, as you read along and follow their magical adventure. Parents and family members will love reading this with their children, grandchildren, siblings, relatives and friends. As you hold this book in your hands, please take the time to delve inside this beautifully crafted tale. Help us to continue to spread the word about the inclusion of every child in storybooks.

Miriam Manderson

Introduction

You have something golden in your hands. This book is a piece of lockdown history, created in the summer of 2020. As a child or an adult, you should feel encouraged by every single page in this book because more than 70 people helped me to manifest this story and bring it to life. It is one of my proudest moments to share with you a vision from God, laid on my heart during my birthday weekend, on the 25th October, 2019. All I needed was faith as small as a mustard seed, to follow the inspired action and dig deep, for the courage to start a Go Fund Me campaign, to produce our first ever community book, for the Look Like Me Book Challenge. When you turn these pages, you are turning over a multitude of collective minds and their concepts.

The Popcorn House was a heart-warming project to be a part of and I am truly glad that God has used me as vessel, to see this vision through to the end.

Always remember the power of foresight, to go forth and create a path in which others will follow. It has been my pleasure to be entrusted with this great story that will be shared on a global scale. Please help us to continue to prioritise the voices of our beautiful, young and talented black and brown authors. This is an integral part of their self-development, ensuring they see positive images of themselves daily. My gratitude, always.

Winsome Duncan

The Popcorn House

Come closer to hear, a story brand new.
Two cousins appear, like fresh morning dew.

"Hi Grandpa, greetings Glam'Ma", they both exclaimed, as they waved goodbye to their parents, down the lane.

Zion's mummy said, "be good, Zion remember you are strong - with a heart of a lion".

The children smiled with excitement and glee.
Unaware of their unexpected journey.

Glam'Ma chuckled, "can you guess what we are going to make? Your favourite, strawberry iced fruit cake".

Glam'Ma's delicious cakes, are the best in town.

Neighbours travelled for miles around, to scoff all her baking treats down.

"Listen up and pay attention to me. We are going to bake a fruit cake, that will be tasty.

Always remember, we MUST work together as a team.

With a splash of vanilla essence, start mixing the butter cream".

Trouble began brewing, as both cousins fought for the wooden spoon.

There was pushing and pulling, then suddenly a loud….

A CRASH and a BANG made a HUGE sound!

Zion and Nevaeh's mixing bowl cracked and fell down.

Glam'Ma's kitchen was covered in flour, when looking all around.

The grandparent's faces were filled with frowns.

The cousins froze on the spot and did not make a sound.

Suddenly, the children gasped, when they saw Grandpa leaning in at the door.
Then Glam'Ma shouted, "NO MORE!"

Grandpa's face was filled with dread. "I agree, it is time for uno bed.

In my house, we work together to achieve our goals and dreams. You have both

demonstrated that you are not a team."

Zion and Nevaeh's faces were filled with regret.

It saddens them to see their beloved grandparents so upset.

Angry words filled the air, as Zion and Nevaeh exchanged cold stares.

"It was my turn to mix the butter cream; sometimes Zion, you can be so mean".

"Nevaeh, you are always mixing the cake; this time I wanted a chance to bake".

Then suddenly their discord was interrupted by a thundering sound. The children stopped arguing and slowly turned around.

In shock, they looked over at the wardrobe and they both could see. It is a beautiful glowing light, shining so pretty.

"Wow, the light is so dazzling bright". Then Zion stepped forth boldly, to investigate.

Nevaeh cried, "no, Zion please wait!" but sadly, she was too late.

The bright light swallowed them into the A-Z zone.

Where no child or adult should ever roam alone.

Boys and girls beware, Zion and Nevaeh had a very big scare.

Did you know The Alphabet Tunnel is real? When your legs turn to jelly, you need a heart of steel.

Whiz-whoosh is all they could hear, as they watched planet earth rapidly disappear.

Letters and words were suspended high in the air. Both their little faces were green with fear.

Glam'Ma always said, "those that do not hear, shall surely feel, the consequences of a bad deal".

Their wise Glam'Ma told them, to work together as a team.
They prayed that they would awake from this terrible dream.

Zion's head was feeling fuzzy and all he wanted was his mummy.
Poor Nevaeh felt scared and sick inside her tummy.

Oh, dear what trouble lay ahead, as letters floated around their heads.
The pair were now filled with anxiety and dread.

BOOM BUMP BANG, finally the two did land, slipping and sliding into the hot, red desert sand.

A soft voice said, "welcome to Kalaria" and they were both in a daze.

When they saw a pink fairy, they stood amazed.

"To escape The Alphabet Tunnel, you were incredibly lucky. Quick get on your feet, for we must hurry!

My name is Ladybug, this is Ducky and Harmony. We are your helpers of destiny.

Gentle Nevaeh for every strand of your hair, I gift to you the Ether Spaceship to carry you through the air. Brave Zion, so bold and strong, surely you will see, my gift of a magical hoodie of invisibility.

'Whiz-Whoosh' will be your code for activation. The path ahead is rough, I wish you guidance and Divine protection.
Follow Ducky and Harmony, they know the way. Be sure to stay on the path and do not stray".

Nevaeh sighed with relief, "oh Ladybug, you are the best, thanks for helping us out of this sticky mess".

Nevaeh stopped and pondered for a while, on how her behaviour had been so wild.

She reached out and said, "Zion, one thing I know to be true, I should have given the wooden spoon to you. Now we are so far from home, I do not know how to right this wrong".

"Sweet Nevaeh, everything is going to be alright.

I promise to get you home by tonight"!

They hugged and were deeply sorry, then looked at Ladybug and said, "we are now ready".

With just one single strand of Nevaeh's hair, the Ether Spaceship began to appear.

"Whiz-Whoosh" are the words they began to say, to take them up, up, up and away.

Ladybug piped up, "Mystic Royal is The Ruler of Kalaria, he is our finest Warrior that I have ever seen. He does not like micro beings, so watch out, he may be mean.

He is your only chance to get back to your family, buckle up and let us hurry".

Mystic Royal was a regal giant. Suddenly, the children knew they had to be compliant.

He stood proud and tall on the Mount Rock, addressing his nation.
Then the sight of the two micros were a cause for a major irritation.

He roared, "how dare you enter into my world".

"You are disobedient boy and a very unruly girl".

Zion remembered what mummy said, that he was strong with a heart of a lion, which was why he was named Zion. So, he spoke up with nerves of iron.

"My bad, for disturbing your meeting, oh great one, we don't want any trouble but we need your assistance to get us back home on the double. An IOU is what I can leave, if you can help us please".

"Very well young Zion, you are now indebted to me; Donny-Dallas and Jellibo come quickly, I know a hidden pathway through the Titan trees".

All the jungle animals ran wild like the wind, as the starry night began to creep in.

"To The Popcorn House, we must go. You better HURRY do not be slow.

There is a warning I must give you, be careful in all that you do.

The house is guarded by Panjiro and the K-bots. If they catch you, they will turn you into a tin bot".

The children looked across at each other and had to think of a marvellous way to not blow their cover.

Donny-Dallas barked with her pink fur flying in the air. "We can only take you to the edge of Bushy Grill, then you are on your own and the rest of the journey is uphill.

We will watch carefully from afar and wish you the best.

Going into The Popcorn House, will be your ultimate test".

"Who goes there? I smell micros near, I am sure that is their footsteps I can hear.

I am Panjiro, the Gate Keeper Guardian of The Popcorn House; no one goes in and no one comes out".

Zion whispered, "I have a brilliant idea, we can go around the side, everyone else go quickly and hide".

As the Popcorn House was their only route back home, they had to work together in unity and not on their own.

Zion carefully whispered, "Whiz-Whoosh" and placed his invisible brown hoodie over their Trinity.

They tiptoed around to the back of the house, quietly.

Little did they know that a K-bot was concealed in Bushy Grill and he raised his arm to sound the alarm. "Intruder alert. Intruders are coming around the back!"

Panjiro looked up with fury and shouted, "Attack!"

There was confusion and a whole heap of stress, as their little hearts were pounding inside their chests.

The cousin's plan was coming together, "Nevaeh, I promise to look after you forever". The Popcorn House was a beautiful scene, with dazzling drinks and remedies that gleamed.

The warm popcorn fire was all aglow, as Panjiro's red laser beam began melting the window.

Ladybug urged the two to drink plenty of any drinks they choose. We have 'self-esteem from within', 'a confidence boost', 'home elixir' and 'power juice'.

Once again, their legs became loose like jelly, as they drank juices and thirst for more splashes in their belly.

"Harmony will follow you back, to make sure you are on the right track".

Nevaeh said, "thanks so much for your help, Ladybug," and gave her a warm, big hug, as Ladybug encourages them, "go ahead, drink up".

Out of The Popcorn House, they had to dash.

The journey home went in a flash.

In Kalaria, the cousins met some fabulous new friends and they secretly hoped they would see them all again.

With Harmony by their side, they were not so frightened.

The Alphabet Tunnel made their senses heighten.

Finally, they were going home to their loving family.

Now understanding the value and ethics of a united community.

They slid down rainbows and bounced on letters and in no time at all, they started to feel much better.

They arrived to find Grandpa and Glam'Ma, sleeping on the settee.

They fell fast asleep while watching telly!

Nevaeh said, "let us plan the greatest surprise.

When they wake up, they will not believe their eyes.

We will bake a cake with strawberries and cream.

This will demonstrate how good we are as a dream team".

Zion smiled at this great idea and the children both grinned from ear to ear.

"You stir Nevaeh, I know it is your favourite thing to do and I'll pour some coconut milk, to make it easy for you".

In no time at all, the kitchen was smelling so nice and the cousins could not wait to have a delicious slice.

The cousins rushed into the front room, "wake up Grandpa, wake up Glam'Ma and come to the balcony.

We have prepared for you an awesome tea party. We wanted to say that we are terribly sorry".

Both grandparents sat for a minute, speechless.

"Come here and give Glam'Ma a big kiss.

The cake looks fantastic and I can see this was made with love; I am happy you found unity, you both deserve a big hug".

Grandpa said, "always remember we are a family, strong and mighty; when we work together, we improve and build our community".

Out of the corner of his eye, Grandpa saw Harmony tweeting at the side. "What a pretty birdy sitting on the rail, I am sure she has one or two fascinating stories to tell".

Zion and Nevaeh chuckled at their adventure, that made them both thrive and gave each other a cool, 'high five'.

THE END

Activities Section

The Popcorn House

KEEP OUT

Poem: Who Am I?

That lion which has a mighty roar throughout the day and a really loud snore, when it hits the hay.

That Leopard which has beautiful camouflaged skin, pouncing on its prey, so it doesn't become thin.

That Rhino which has a great big horn, defending its family from harm, from sunrise to dawn.

Or maybe the Buffalo which has a big strong crown, always being silly when no one's around.

That Elephant with that massive brain, no matter its size, always climbing the highest mountains.

It's that boy who's from the tropical Caribbean, swimming in the sea like a funny amphibian.

It is that girl, who's from sunny Africa,
Dancing around like an acrobatic cheerleader.
Can you guess who I am?
I am all the young black boys and girls of this world!

By Ben Lee

Poem: Who Am I?

Now it is your turn to write your very own Who Am I? Poem.

Enjoy.

1_____

2_____

3_____

4_____

5_____

6_____

7_____

8_____

9_____

10_____

11_____

12_____

Children of the Sun

Chorus:

We are children of the sun; our lives have just begun.

We're the chosen ones. We are talented by far.

We are shining stars, who know who we are.

Verse 1:

Always believe in your dreams. Even when others are mean. You can achieve great things. If you think you can win.

Chorus:

We are children of the sun; our lives have just begun.

We're the chosen ones. We are talented by far.

We are shining stars, who know who we are.

Verse 2:

Be kind and help if you can. Make sure that you understand. Life is for sharing and caring. Make sure you're always giving.

We are children of the sun, children of the sun, children of the sun x 2.

Winsome Duncan © 2010

Epilogue

Well done for making it to the end of what was truly an amazing journey for me. I trust in you to pass this story on to family and friends. It deeply affected me to see that only 1% of Black, Asian and Minority Ethnic main characters were represented in children's storybooks within the UK, according to the findings of the Centre of Learning for Primary Education.

I knew then that I had to be part of the solution. As you can see, we told a story that conveyed our abilities in a positive light. We want to continue on this path and work with our second cohort, of 13 – 18 year olds. Yet, we know we cannot do this without your support, as our team are currently all volunteers. If you can champion our cause, then please visit and share our 'Look Like Me Book Challenge' Go Fund Me page and make a generous donation. This will enable us to continue to plant positive seeds in the minds of our young black and brown budding authors.

It is about time we let them know that their stories are valuable and worthy to be told, visit here:

www.gofundme.com/f/look-like-me-book-challenge.

43

About the Author

Meet Winsome Duncan, who is a Book Confidence Coach and an award-winning entrepreneur. As the Founder of Peaches Publications, her book publishing experience spans more than a decade and she is passionate about books. Winsome is a number 1 best-selling author with an amazing 15 books in her repertoire. Winsome's written television work has featured on BBC iPlayer, SKY, Virgin TV and BBC London radio.

As a motivational speaker, Winsome was trained by public figure, Les Brown and has also trained with the UK's top speaker, Andy Harrington. Winsome's books are highly acclaimed, having received national press and media coverage and Winsome has been endorsed by former Minister of Justice, Sir Simon Hughes. Winsome resides in London, England and says writing is her passion and purpose in life. She continues to aspire to inspire her community to write and tell their stories. To make contact, simply visit www.looklikeme.co.uk or www.peachespublications.co.uk.

Meet the Co-Authors

A HUGE thank you to all the parents and guardians who took the time to ensure their child or children were involved in the Look Like Me Book Challenge. All of our authors did so well and we would like you to join us in a massive congratulations, as we introduce you to them:

A Bischof, Kayla-Mai Alvares, Ryleigh Benson, Jahzara Mckie, Omari Bailey, Ayana Bailey, Khalisah Catoja, Theo Duncan, Cameron Duncan, Imayah Dayes, Nathan Uzor, Rinnah Uzor, Dilan Ignacio, Sam-Jay Robinson, Zayan Montgomery Smith, Iman Montgomery Smith, Isis Montgomery Smith, Jihad Montgomery Smith, Saniah, Malia, Jeremiah Yates and Kylah-Angel Macauley.

To respect the privacy of our parents' wishes, some of our parents have omitted their child/children's names. The co-authors listed will be joining us on our press and media national campaign and parental permission has been granted.

Meet The Facilitators

Black Inspired Colouring Book